Sam at the Seaside

Written by **Mary Labatt**

Illustrated by **Marisol Sarrazin**

Kids Can Press

® Kids Can Read is a registered trademark of Kids Can Press Ltd.

Text © 2006 Mary Labatt
Illustrations © 2006 Marisol Sarrazin

Kids Can Press acknowledges the financial support of the Government of Ontario, through the Ontario Media Development Corporation's Ontario Book Initiative; the Ontario Arts Council; the Canada Council for the Arts; and the Government of Canada, through the BPIDP, for our publishing activity.

Published in Canada by
Kids Can Press Ltd.
29 Birch Avenue
Toronto, ON M4V 1E2

Published in the U.S. by
Kids Can Press Ltd.
2250 Military Road
Tonawanda, NY 14150

www.kidscanpress.com

Edited by Jennifer Stokes
Designed by Marie Bartholomew
Printed and bound in China

The hardcover edition of this book is smyth sewn casebound.
The paperback edition of this book is limp sewn with a drawn-on cover.

CM 06 0 9 8 7 6 5 4 3 2 1
CM PA 06 0 9 8 7 6 5 4 3 2 1

Library and Archives Canada Cataloguing in Publication

Labatt, Mary, [date]

    Sam at the seaside / written by Mary Labatt ; illustrated by Marisol Sarrazin.

(Kids Can read)

ISBN-13: 978-1-55337-876-1 (bound) ISBN-13: 978-1-55337-877-8 (pbk.)
ISBN-10: 1-55337-876-8 (bound) ISBN-10: 1-55337-877-6 (pbk.)

I. Sarrazin, Marisol, 1965– II. Title. III. Series: Kids Can read (Toronto, Ont.)

PS8573.A135S23 2006   jC813'.54   C2005-906425-0

Kids Can Press is a *corus*™ Entertainment company

Joan and Bob were making sandwiches.

Bob made egg sandwiches.

Joan made peanut butter sandwiches.

"Yum!" thought Sam.

Joan got a big basket.

Bob put the sandwiches in the basket.

"Come on, Sam," said Joan.

"We are going to the seaside."

"What is the seaside?" thought Sam.

"Why does it need sandwiches?"

Joan and Bob got in the car.

Sam got in, too.

They drove out of town.

They drove past fields and farms.

6

Sam stuck her nose in the air.

She smelled something.

"Is that the seaside?" she thought.

"This is the seaside, Sam," said Joan.

Sam saw water and sand.

She saw seagulls and boats

and people and dogs.

"Wow!" thought Sam.

"I can have fun here!"

Joan and Bob sat on the blanket.

They ate sandwiches.

"Woof!" said Sam.

"Sandwiches are not for puppies,"

said Joan.

"Hmph," thought Sam.

"I need to have fun," thought Sam.

She ran to the water.

She walked in the water
just like the people.

Sam did not see a big wave coming.

SPLASH!

The wave hit Sam!

Sam saw some kids making a sandcastle.

"That looks like fun," she thought.

"I will do that."

Sam ran to the sandcastle.

She dug in the sand just like the kids.

She dug and dug.

Sam did not see where the sand was going.

"Stop puppy!" yelled the kids.

"Go away, puppy!"

Sam saw some crabs digging in the sand.

"That looks like fun," she thought.

"I will do that."

Sam ran to the crabs.

She put her nose down to sniff them.

Sam did not see a big crab coming.

The crab pinched Sam's nose.

"YOW!" said Sam.

Sam was wet and her nose hurt.

"I am having a bad time," she thought.

"I need to have fun."

Sam sat down.

"It is not fun to walk in the water.

It is not fun to make a sandcastle.

It is not fun to look at the crabs,"

she thought.

Then Sam saw a hot dog.

"Yum!" she thought.

"Awk!" said a seagull.

The seagull flew down

and grabbed the hot dog.

Sam saw an ice-cream cone.

"Yum!" she thought.

"Awk!" said a seagull.

The seagull flew down
and grabbed the cone.

"I am having a bad time," thought Sam.

"I do not like the seaside.

The seaside is not for puppies."

Then Sam saw something on the sand.

"Mmm," thought Sam.

"This is a good smell."

She poked the thing with her nose.

It did not move.

"Good," she thought.

"This thing will not bite me."

Sam sniffed and sniffed.

"Mmm-mmmm," she thought.

"I LOVE this smell!"

Sam rolled on the sand.

"Now I am having fun!" she thought.

"Oh, no!" yelled Joan.

"Oh, no!" yelled Bob.

"That is stinky!" yelled Joan.

"Stop, Sam! Stop!" yelled Bob.

Sam did not hear Joan and Bob.

She loved the fish smell.

She rolled and rolled.

"Awk!!" said a seagull.

He dived at Sam.

"AWK!!! AWK!!!

AWK!!! AWK!!!"

Sam ran to the blanket.

The seagull dived and dived.

Sam tried to hide under the blanket.

"Yikes!" yelled Joan.

"Yikes!" yelled Bob.

"You smell bad!" yelled Joan.

"Off the blanket!" yelled Bob.

Joan and Bob packed up.

They took the blanket.

They took the basket.

They held their noses.

"You stink, Sam," they said.

"I do not stink," thought Sam.

"I smell wonderful!"